P9-DDS-294

Martina
love,
Nana + Great Granfey
2007

Favorite Fairy Tales

and Fables

Written by Peter Holeinone
Illustrated by Tony Wolf

Adapted from works by
Aesop, Jean de la Fontaine, The Brothers Grimm,
Hans Christian Andersen, Carlo Collodi,
Alexander Afanasjev, Giambattista Basile,
Giovanni Boccaccio, and Robert Browning

★ A Tell-Me-A-Story Keepsake Treasury ★

Favorite Fairy Tales
and Fables

Dalmatian Press

FAVORITE FAIRY TALES *and* FABLES
Copyright © 2004 Dami International, Milano

All rights reserved
Printed in China

Editor: Louise Gikow
Cover Design: Emily Robertson

Published in 2004 by Dalmatian Press, LLC.
The DALMATIAN PRESS name and logo are trademarks
of Dalmatian Press, LLC, Franklin, Tennessee 37067.
No part of this book may be reproduced or copied in any form
without the written permission of Dalmatian Press.

ISBN: 1-40370-770-7
13312-0604

04 05 06 07 SFO 10 9 8 7 6 5 4 3 2 1

Tell Me A Story.

When you read a story to your child, lots of good things happen. You show your child that reading is exciting and fun. You encourage the growth and development not just of your little one's imagination but also his or her vocabulary, comprehension skills, and overall school readiness.

Research shows, time and time again, that children who are read to on a regular basis do significantly better in school than children who are not read to at home. We encourage you to spend ten to twenty minutes every day reading to your child. It's a small amount of quality time that reaps a big reward!

It's also important to keep reading books *to* your child and *with* your child even after he or she is reading independently. You can share books that are slightly more difficult than what your child is reading on his or her own because you are available to help with vocabulary words and any questions your child may have about the story.

Read and Discuss.

No matter how old your child is, or how well she is reading independently, remember that story time is the perfect opportunity to talk about what you're reading and any other topics that might arise from it. This kind of dialog helps make stories come alive and adds depth to your child's reading experience.

What would you do if you were in the story? you might ask. *How might you fix this problem? Did the character do the right thing?* and so forth.

Your child's Keepsake Treasury includes dialogic questions throughout the stories to prompt meaningful and memorable conversations. Ask your own questions as well. You might be surprised at the imaginative discussions that follow. You can learn more about dialogic reading online at: *http://www.readingrockets.org.*

We hope that *Favorite Fairy Tales and Fables* will become a treasured part of your family's library.

Happy Reading!

CONTENTS

THE THREE LITTLE PIGS

Once upon a time, there were three little pigs who left their home to see the world.

All summer long, they roamed through the woods and over the plains. They played games and had lots of fun. But when autumn came, they decided they needed their own homes.

Each pig had a different idea of what that home should be.

The first little pig was the laziest, and he decided to build a house of straw.

"It will only take a day," he said.

The other two pigs thought this was a very bad idea.

"A house made of straw will be weak," they told him. "It will fall down during the first rainstorm."

But the first little pig refused to listen. He built his house out of straw.

If you were building a house, what would you make your house out of?

The second little pig was not so lazy. He decided to build his house out of twigs. It took him three days.

"You've worked much too hard!" said the first little pig. "My house of straw was much easier to make."

"You haven't worked hard enough!" said the third little pig. "It takes time, patience, and hard work to build a house that is strong enough to stand up to wind, rain, and snow."

The third little pig built his house out of bricks. It was the strongest, sturdiest house in the neighborhood.

And that was a good thing.

Because one day, a big, bad wolf came to town. And he was very, very hungry.

He decided to visit the houses of the three little pigs.

The big, bad wolf came to the house of the first little pig. It was made of straw.

"Little pig, little pig, let me in!" he cried.

"Not by the hair of my chinny chin chin!" the little pig answered.

"Then I'll huff and I'll puff and I'll blow your house in!" said the wolf.

And that's exactly what he did.

Luckily, the first little pig escaped. He ran to the house of the second little pig.

The big, bad wolf then came to the house of the second little pig. It was made of twigs.

"Little pig, little pig, let me in!" he cried.

"Not by the hair of my chinny chin chin!" the little pig answered.

"Then I'll huff and I'll puff and I'll blow your house in!" said the wolf.

And that's exactly what he did.

Luckily, the two little pigs escaped. They ran to the house of the third little pig.

"The big, bad wolf is coming!" they cried. "Let us in!"
The third little pig opened the door wide.
His two brothers got inside just in time.

The big, bad wolf came to the house of the third little pig.
It was made of bricks.

"Little pig, little pig, let me in!" he cried.

"Not by the hair of my chinny chin chin!" the third little
pig answered.

"Then I'll huff and I'll puff and I'll blow your house in!" said the wolf.

And that's exactly what the wolf tried to do.

But he couldn't. The brick house was too strong.

So the wolf decided to go down the chimney.

Uh-oh! There's a wolf coming down the chimney! What would you do?

The third little pig was very clever. He had already started a fire in the fireplace.

And when the big, bad wolf came down the chimney, he had a very hot time indeed.

He scampered back up the chimney and was gone in a flash.

And that was the end of the big, bad wolf!

The three happy little pigs danced round and round the yard, singing:

Tra-la-la! Tra-la-la!
The big, bad wolf will never come back!
His tail is burned and his coat singed black!
Tra-la-la! Tra-la-la!

And they lived happily ever after—in three brick houses.

THE CRAB AND THE HERON

Once upon a time, there was an old heron—a big, blue bird with a long, skinny neck. He made his home near a beautiful pond. He was stiff and slow because of his age, and he had trouble catching fish for his lunch.

So he decided to use his wits.

He went to a crab who was known as a great chatterbox.

"I have heard some terrible news," he said. "Soon, fishermen will be coming to the pond with their nets. They're going to take away all the fish! I'll have no more meals. And all the fish will end up in a frying pan!"

The crab quickly scuttled away to the bank of the pond. He told the fish the awful news.

The frightened fish begged the crab for good advice. He had none to give. So he returned to the old blue heron.

"The fish are scared stiff," he told the heron. "They don't know what to do. You snap up a few fish yourself now and again, so it's in your best interest to help the fish survive. Without the fish, you will go hungry. So what shall we do?"

> *Do you think the crab and the fish can trust the heron to help? Why or why not?*

The heron pretended to think for a moment. Then he lifted his beak into the air and said, "I'll tell you what! I can carry the fish to a pond hidden in the forest. They'll be quite safe there. But will they trust me?"

The fish were so scared of the fishermen that they agreed to this strange offer.

So the heron began his trips between the pond and the forest. Each time, he carried one or two of the fish in his beak.

But the crab soon noticed that the heron was taking longer and longer to fly to the hidden pond. The crab also noticed that the heron's tummy was getting a good deal plumper.

Days later, when all the fish had been rescued from the pond, the heron asked the crab, "Do you want to be rescued, too?"

"Certainly," replied the crab. "Bend over. I'll climb on your neck. I hate to make your beak tired!"

When they were far from the pond, the crab noticed that the ground was littered with fish bones. He now knew the truth.

The heron had not been saving the fish. He had been eating the fish himself! And the crab knew, too, that if the heron had his way, the crab was about to become the heron's next meal.

So he clung tightly to the heron's neck with his strong claws.

"I have no intention of coming to the same bad end as the fish," he told the bird. "Just put me gently into the water. I'm not letting go of your neck until I feel safe!"

The heron was forced to do as the crab asked. He was quite annoyed, since he had been looking forward to crab for supper.

And that is why, to this day, crabs and herons do not get along.

THE WOLF AND THE SEVEN KIDS

Once upon a time, a Mother Goat lived in a pretty little house with her seven kids.

She often had to leave home to do the shopping. And she always gave her children the same warnings before she set off to market.

"Don't open the door to anyone," she would say. "There is a big, bad wolf lurking in the neighborhood. He has horrible claws and a deep, growly voice. If he knocks, keep the door tightly shut. Don't forget!"

"We won't, Mother," said the seven little kids.

Mother Goat's fears about the big, bad wolf were well founded. As she was greeting one of her neighbors on her way to go shopping, the wolf, disguised as a peasant, was hiding close by, listening to every word.

"Good. Very good," said the wolf to himself. "Mother Goat is going shopping. While she is at the market, I'll drop by her house and gobble up her kids!"

In every house, there are rules we have to follow. What are some of your rules? Do you follow them all the time?

When he saw Mother Goat disappear down the road, the wolf hurried along to her house. There, he threw off his disguise.

He then growled in a deep voice, "Open the door! Open the door! It's Mother! I've just come back from the market. Open the door!"

The seven kids heard the wolf calling. They heard his deep voice. And they remembered what Mother Goat had said.

"We know who you are!" they called. "You're the wolf! Our mother has a sweet, gentle voice, not a deep, growly one like yours. Go away! We'll never open the door for you!"

The wolf was very, very angry. But then he had an idea.

He dashed off to the baker's shop. There, he got a big cake, dripping with honey. He thought the honey would help sweeten his deep, growly voice. And in fact, when he had finished the cake, his voice didn't sound quite so deep any more.

He practiced imitating Mother Goat's voice. You see, he had heard it in the woods.

Then, when he sounded just like Mother Goat, he raced back to the house of the seven kids.

Can you imitate someone's voice? Whose? Show me!

"Open the door! Open the door! It's Mother!" he cried. "I've just come back from the market. Open the door!"

The wolf's voice really did sound a lot like Mother Goat's. The kids were just about to open the door when the gray kid shook his head. The gray kid was the youngest and the smallest, but he was also the smartest one of all.

"Mother, let us see your foot!" he cried.

Without thinking, the wolf raised a black, hairy paw.

"You're not our mother!" cried the kids. "She doesn't have black, hairy paws! Go away, you wicked wolf!"

And once more, the wolf had to leave hungry.

"Black, hairy paws?" the wolf growled to himself. "We'll see about that!"

He ran down to the mill and found a sack of flour. Then he thrust his paws into the flour until they were pure white.

"I'll trick them this time," he said. "Mmmm! I can't wait to gobble up those kids!"

Why did the wolf cover his paws in flour? Is there ever a time when it's okay to trick someone else?

When the wolf got back to the house of the seven kids, he called out once again.

"Open the door! Open the door! It's Mother!" he cried. "I've just come back from the market. Open the door!"

"Mother, let us see your foot!" cried the wary kids.

The wily wolf lifted a snow white paw. Reassured, the kids threw open the door.

It was a big mistake.

There was the wolf, his teeth sharp and glistening, his claws pointy and long. He growled fiercely. The little kids scattered in terror.

One hid under the table while another crawled beneath the bed. A third hid in the cupboard and the fourth tried to hide in the oven. The fifth crouched

inside a barrel and the sixth hid in a basket. The seventh—the little gray kid—hid in the grandfather clock.

But one by one, the wolf found them all and gobbled them up.

The only kid to escape was the little gray kid. The wolf never imagined that there was room for a kid inside the grandfather clock.

 Can you find the hidden kids? Where would you hide to escape the big, bad wolf?

When Mother Goat came back from the market and saw that the door was ajar, she despaired. What she had feared had come to pass.

She dropped into a chair, sobbing bitterly.

But as she cried, the door to the grandfather clock swung open. Out ran the little gray kid!

"Mommy! Mommy! It was terrible!" the little gray kid cried. "The wolf came, and I think he's eaten all my brothers!"

"My poor child!" sobbed Mother Goat. "Are you the only one left?"

"Let's go search outside—please, Mother?" the little gray kid begged. And so Mother Goat and her kid went out into the garden.

There, they heard somebody snoring. It was the greedy wolf. His feast of kids had been too much for him, and he had fallen fast asleep.

In a flash, Mother Goat had an idea.

"Hurry to the house," she told her littlest kid. "Fetch me a needle and thread and a pair of scissors!"

The little gray kid did as he was told.

Quickly, Mother Goat cut open the wolf's stomach. As she had hoped, the terrible beast had swallowed each kid whole. There they all were, still alive in his tummy. One by one, they popped out.

"Shhh," said Mother Goat. "Not a sound. Quick—fetch me some stones!"

They filled the wolf's stomach with stones and stitched it up again. Then they hid behind some bushes to see what would happen. When the wolf woke up, he was very, very thirsty.

"What a heavy tummy I have!" he said. "I've eaten too much. I need a drink of water."

Now the wolf is being tricked! Was it okay for Mother Goat to trick the wolf? Why?

The wolf went to the river to drink. But his tummy was so full of heavy stones that he tipped over and fell into the water.

The weight took him straight to the bottom. Mother Goat and her kids jumped with joy as he sank.

And the wicked wolf never bothered anyone again.

THE CITY MOUSE AND THE COUNTRY MOUSE

Once upon a time, a city mouse went to visit his cousin in the country.

They spent the day together and had a wonderful time.

The country mouse showed his city cousin the beauties of nature—the bluebells and the daisies, the butterflies and ladybugs.

And he showed him the delicious food a mouse could find if he was clever. There were hazelnuts and fruits in the meadow. There were crunchy vegetables from neighboring gardens.

The city mouse was used to much finer fare. But he had a wonderful time.

And to say thank-you to his country cousin, he invited the country mouse to visit him in his big-city home.

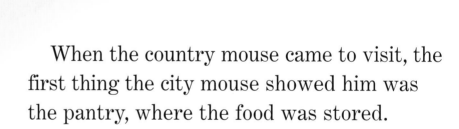

When the country mouse came to visit, the
first thing the city mouse showed him was
the pantry, where the food was stored.

The country mouse was amazed.

"I've never seen anything like it!" he said.
"Are all these wonderful things for eating?"

"Of course," came the reply. "Be my guest!"

So the two started to feast. The country mouse tried not to stuff himself, but it was hard. Everything tasted so good!

"You're the luckiest mouse I've ever met!" said the country mouse.

Do you think the city mouse is lucky? What do you think a city mouse's favorite food would be? What's your favorite food?

Suddenly, the country mouse heard the sound of heavy footsteps.

"Run for it!" the city mouse whispered. And they ran just in time. For there, within an inch of them, was the lady of the house's large foot.

What a fright!

Luckily, the lady went away again, so the mice could continue their feast. But the country mouse's appetite was not quite what it had been before.

"Don't worry!" his city cousin told him. "She's gone. Now for the honey. Have you ever tasted honey?"

"Yes, once, a long time ago," the country mouse replied. (He was trying to sound like a mouse of the world, for, actually, he had never tasted honey at all.)

"Well, taste some more!" the city mouse urged.

And when he did… oh, my! It was sweet and gooey and so good!

"I've never tasted anything so delicious in my whole life!" the country mouse exclaimed.

Suddenly, there came the sound of footsteps once again, thumping down the hall.

By now, the country mouse knew what this meant, and he raced for a hiding place. The city mouse was close behind.

The man of the house had come to fetch some bottles.

When he saw the spilled honey, he groaned, "Those mice! I thought they were gone for good! I'll send the cat."

Even after the man had left the pantry, the mice trembled with fear. It was not only the man's sudden visit that had given them a fright. It was the words: "I'll send the cat."

And sure enough, soon after, the mice heard a creaking sound. Out of the dim light glowed a pair of horrid yellow eyes. Then the country mouse saw it was a large cat!

The country mouse was sure that the cat could hear the beating of his heart. He covered his ears and tried to forget the cat.

"Be calm. Nothing will happen to us. We are safe hidden away here."

And luckily, he was right. The cat discovered a juicy bit of sausage on the floor and forgot all about the mice. After he had eaten it, he was full, so he padded out to take a nap.

As soon as the cat left and the danger was past, the country mouse shook his city cousin's paw.

"Thanks so much for everything," he told the city mouse. "But I must rush off! I can't stand all these shocks.

"I'd rather sit down to a simple meal of a few acorns in peace than face a spread of delicious food with danger all around. I'm going home."

And that's exactly what he did.

> *If you were a mouse, would you want to live in the city or the country? Why?*

THE ADVENTURES OF TOM THUMB

Once upon a time, a giant quarreled with a greedy wizard over sharing a treasure.

After the fight, the giant was very angry indeed.

"Get out of my sight before I crush you with my thumb!" he told the wizard.

The wizard was no fool. He knew the giant could do it. So he waited until he was a safe distance away, and then he placed a terrible spell on the giant.

"Your wife is about to have a baby," the wizard said. "May your son never grow any taller than my own thumb!"

And sure enough… a little while later, the giant's wife gave birth to a tiny baby. They called him Tom Thumb.

Tom's parents had a hard time with Tom. They could never find him, because he was so small. They had to speak in whispers for fear of deafening him.

And although Tom loved his parents, he was much happier playing with small creatures like himself. He rode piggyback on the snail and danced with the ladybugs. Even though he was tiny, he had a wonderful time.

One day, Tom was visiting his froggy friend when he had some terrible luck. A big fish came by and swallowed him up!

But the fish had bad luck, too. A little later, the king's fisherman caught him on a hook. He ended up in the royal kitchen, being cut open by the royal cook.

Wasn't the cook surprised when out of the fish stepped Tom Thumb, quite alive and none the worse for his adventure!

"What am I going to do with him?" the cook wondered. Then he had an idea. "He can be a royal page! And I know exactly how to introduce him to the king!"

The cook baked a cake that looked like a castle. Then he put Tom Thumb inside.

When the cake was served to the king and his court, Tom Thumb stepped across the chocolate drawbridge, blowing on a tiny trumpet.

The guests clapped excitedly at the cook's skill, and the king was the most excited of all. He rewarded the cook with a bag of gold and made Tom Thumb a permanent page in his court.

Tom was given a white mouse to ride and a gold pin for a sword. He ate at the king's table and fed on the king's food.

In exchange, at banquets he would march up and down the table, entertaining the guests with his trumpet.

He was very happy.

> *Tom must have had fun doing his job. What do you think would be the most fun job? Why?*

But there was someone at court who was not happy, and that was the court cat. The cat had been the king's pet, but now that Tom was there, the cat was forgotten.

So the jealous cat decided to ambush Tom in the garden and make him run away.

Rather than running away, however, Tom whipped out his gold pin. He stabbed at the cat until the frightened animal ran away.

Oh, the cat was angry! So he decided to use trickery to end Tom's career at court.

One night, he meowed to the king, "Sire! Be on your guard. There is a plot against your life!" And then he told a terrible lie. "Tom Thumb is going to poison your food!"

Now, the king didn't want to be poisoned. So he threw Tom Thumb into prison. Actually, because Tom was so tiny, he threw him into the case of a clock.

Tom was there for a long time, swinging back and forth on the pendulum.

One night, Tom saw a moth flying around the room.

"Let me out, please!" Tom said, tapping on the glass. And the moth took pity on Tom and released him.

"I will take you to the Butterfly Kingdom, where everyone is tiny like yourself," the moth told him. "You will be safe there."

And that is what happened. To this very day, if you are in the Butterfly Kingdom, you can see the statue Tom built to thank the moth for rescuing him!

GOLDILOCKS AND THE THREE BEARS

Once upon a time, in a large forest, there lived three bears—a Papa Bear, a Mama Bear, and a Baby Bear.

Each bear had his own bowl for porridge. There was a large bowl for the Papa Bear, a medium-sized bowl for the Mama Bear, and a little bowl for the Baby Bear.

Each bear had his own chair, too. There was a large chair for the Papa Bear, a medium-sized chair for the Mama Bear, and a little chair for the Baby Bear.

And each bear had his own bed. There was a large bed for the Papa Bear, a medium-sized bed for the Mama Bear, and a little bed for the Baby Bear.

One day, Mama Bear cooked up some porridge for the bears' breakfast. But the porridge was too hot to eat.

"Let us take a walk in the woods until the porridge cools," Papa Bear suggested. Mama Bear and Baby Bear thought that was a very good idea.

So Mama Bear tied on her blue bonnet and picked up her gray shawl. Papa Bear put on his red and blue waistcoat with his blue hat. Baby Bear put on his new blue sweater. And the three bears went out for a walk in the woods.

While the bears were out walking, a little girl named Goldilocks wandered nearby. She was busy picking flowers when she drew near to the house of the three bears.

"What a lovely house," she thought. "I wonder if anyone is home. I'm hungry and thirsty, and perhaps whoever lives there will give me some food and drink."

Goldilocks went up to the cottage and knocked on the door. She knocked again, and then again. But no one answered.

Then she tried the door, and it opened.

"I think I'll take a peek inside," she decided.

The first thing Goldilocks saw when she entered the cottage were the three bowls of porridge, sitting on the table.

"Mmmm," she said. "Porridge! And I'm so hungry—I think I'll have a bite."

She tasted the porridge in Papa Bear's bowl. But it was too hot.

She tasted the porridge in Mama Bear's bowl. But it was too cold.

Then she tasted the porridge in Baby Bear's bowl. And it was just right. So she ate it all up!

After she finished the porridge, Goldilocks started to feel a little tired.

"I think I'll sit down for a little while," she thought. "Picking flowers is hard work!"

She tried Papa Bear's chair, but it was too hard.

She tried Mama Bear's chair, but it was too soft.

Then she tried Baby Bear's chair. And it was just right!

Goldilocks sat down. But the little chair could not take the weight of a girl. It broke, and she crashed to the floor!

Goldilocks decided to go upstairs and see what she could find.

She found herself in the bears' bedroom.

"Ahhh!" she yawned. "I would like a bit of a rest. After all, picking flowers is *very* hard work!"

She lay down in Papa Bear's bed, but it was too hard.

She lay down in Mama Bear's bed, but it was too soft.

Finally, she lay down in Baby Bear's bed. And it was just right.

It was so comfy and so cozy, in fact, that she decided to lie there for just another minute. Another minute passed, and then another.

For you see, Goldilocks had fallen fast asleep.

Soon after, the bears came back from their walk in the woods.

"Oh, no!" Papa Bear said. "Somebody has been eating my porridge!"

"Somebody has been eating my porridge!" said Mama Bear.

"Somebody has been eating my porridge, too," said Baby Bear. "And it's all gone!"

"And look!" Mama Bear added. "Somebody has been sitting in my chair."

"Somebody has been sitting in my chair," Papa Bear said.

"Somebody has been sitting in my chair, too," Baby Bear cried. "And it's broken all to pieces!"

Then the bears went upstairs.

"Look!" said Papa Bear. "Somebody has been sleeping in my bed."

"Somebody has been sleeping in my bed," said Mama Bear.

"Somebody has been sleeping in my bed, too," whispered Baby Bear. "And she's there right now!"

That's when Goldilocks woke up.

She was so surprised to see three bears standing at the foot of the bed that she gave a little shriek, popped out of Baby Bear's bed as fast as a wink, and ran out of the house as quickly as her feet could carry her.

And that was the last the bears saw of Goldilocks... and the last Goldilocks saw of the three bears!

THE HARE AND THE HEDGEHOG

Once upon a time, there was an old hedgehog who lived in the woods with his twin sons.

The twins loved apples, and they liked nothing more than an apple feast.

But the father hedgehog also loved turnips. So every so often, his two sons raided the neighbor's vegetable patch for some nice, juicy ones.

One day, one of the hedgehogs was in the vegetable garden, behind a large cabbage, when out popped a hare.

"Rather late, aren't you?" said the hare. "I've been here for hours. Are you always so slow? If you're not careful, the farmer will catch you for sure!"

Now, hedgehogs are, in fact, slow animals. But nobody likes to be teased. So the hedgehog decided to get his revenge. You see, he had an idea…

"I can run faster than you if I try," he said.

The hare laughed and laughed.

"You?" he chortled. "Run faster than me? Why, my father and my grandfather were the swiftest hares in the forest! Grandfather even won a gold penny in a race with all the other hares. And you say you can run faster than me?

"Well, I bet my grandpa's gold penny that I can win a race with you without even trying! What will you give me if I win?"

"All our apple harvest," the hedgehog said.

"You're on," declared the hare.

"All right," the hedgehog said quietly. "I'll meet you in the plowed field tomorrow morning when the sun rises. We'll race to the end of the field. And you'll see exactly how fast I can be!"

The next morning, the hedgehog was waiting in the field when the hare arrived.

"I'll just take off my overalls," the hare said, "so I can run faster."

"Are you ready?" the hedgehog asked.

"You bet!" said the hare.

Three... two... one... and the race was on!

The hare streaked to the end of the field like a bolt of lightning... only to find the hedgehog there waiting for him. And the hedgehog wasn't even out of breath!

"Rather late, aren't you?" said the hedgehog. "I've been here for hours."

The hare couldn't believe his eyes.

"Let's race again," he gasped.

Two more times, they ran the race. But each time, the hedgehog was waiting for the hare at the end of the field.

Finally, the hare had to admit that the hedgehog was faster. So he handed over the gold penny to the hedgehog.

How do you think the hedgehog won the race?

When the hedgehog got home at the end of the day, a party was held at his home.

Father Hedgehog played the accordion, and the two twin brothers danced.

"Congratulations on winning the race!" said one hedgehog brother to the other.

"No, congratulations to *you* for winning the race!" his brother said.

They both laughed. For, you see, they had both run the race.

Hedgehogs aren't very fast, but they are quick thinkers. When the hare had boasted about how fast he could run, the hedgehog had come up with a plan.

Each time he and the hare had run the race, his brother had stood at the finish line, pretending to be him. So it was really the two brothers who had been racing the hare—not just one!

And the hare never did find out how the hedgehog managed to beat him.

THE HARE AND THE ELEPHANT.

Once upon a time, there was a baby elephant and his playmate, a very large hare.

They were great friends and played many games together. The elephant pulled down big bunches of bananas for his snacks. The hare ate bright red carrots. They both had a wonderful time.

One day, the hare said to the elephant, "Who do you think is bigger—you or me?"

The elephant laughed and laughed.

"You must be joking!" he said. "I am an elephant. You are a rabbit. Even on tiptoe, you stand no higher than my knee!"

The hare shook his head. "I'm not so sure," he said. "I think we need someone to judge the matter, since I say I'm bigger than you."

"You can have any judge you want," said the elephant.

"Then let us go to the village of the people and see what they have to say," said the hare. And they did.

As they walked toward the village, they met some of the people who lived there.

"Ah, look at the baby elephant," one man said. "Isn't he small and cute?"

"Yes, he is," said a woman. "But he will soon grow up."

Then the people noticed the hare.

"What a big hare!" said a girl. "That is the biggest hare I have ever seen!"

"Look at his paws! Look at his ears! He is surely a giant among hares!" a boy agreed.

Well, no sooner had the rabbit heard this than he turned to his friend.

"We can go home now!" he said. "You have heard the people. I'm big and you're small."

The elephant shook his head. Then he laughed. After all, his friend had beaten him—even if it was through trickery.

"All right, all right, you win," he said. "But be careful to stay out of my way. For if you don't, a small elephant like me could crush a big hare like you under his foot!"

The hare was very careful from then on.

THE TORTOISE AND THE HARE

Once upon a time, there was a hare who boasted that he could run faster than anyone else. He spent all his time teasing a poor old tortoise for its slowness.

Finally, the tortoise could take no more.

"Who do you think you are?" the tortoise said. "You may be fast, but even the fastest can be beaten!"

The hare laughed and laughed. "Beaten? Me? I don't think so."

"Then I challenge you to a race," the tortoise said. "And may the best animal win!"

A course was set, and the next day, the tortoise and the hare met at the starting line.

"Ready… set… go!" said the hedgehog.

The tortoise started off. He was so slow that the hare said to himself, "I have plenty of time. I think I'll go have some breakfast!"

The tortoise just trudged on.

The hare went off to munch some carrots and cabbages he had seen in a nearby field.

When he was done, he was sleepy.

"I'm sure I have time for a little nap," he said. "That tortoise is barely halfway done with the race."

So the hare lay down under a bush.

His tummy was full and the sun was hot. Soon, the hare was dreaming of racing past the tortoise.

Suddenly, he woke up. He peered down the road.

And there was the tortoise—only a few feet from the finish line!

The hare bounded up and went running after him. But it was too late.

The lazy hare had lost. The tortoise had won.

"Slow but steady wins the race," the tortoise told him.

And the hare never boasted about his speed ever again.

SNOW WHITE

Once upon a time, there was a little girl whose father was the king of a far-away land. Her name was Snow White.

She lived happily in the palace for many years. She was a gentle child and loved flowers and nature.

Sadly, one day her mother died. And her father took a new wife.

The new queen was a very vain woman, who spent much time looking into her mirror.

Now, this mirror was magic. And if you looked into it, it would always tell the truth.

The queen used this mirror every day. Each morning, she would ask it, "Mirror, tell me the truth. Who is the fairest lady in the land?"

For many years, the mirror had replied, "You are, my Lady. You are the fairest."

But as Snow White grew older, she became more and more beautiful. And one day, the mirror answered, "You are very beautiful, O Queen. But Snow White is more beautiful than you!"

The queen flew into a rage. She called her woodsman to her.

"I want you to take Snow White into the forest," the queen ordered. "And once you are there, I want you to put her to death!"

The woodsman was frightened of the queen. But he also loved Snow White. Everyone did.

His heart was heavy as he took Snow White deep into the woods. But there, rather than end her life, he ran off and let her live.

Snow White, saddened and terrified, stayed in the forest for a night and a day.

Then, realizing that the woodsman would not return, she began to wander through the trees.

She came upon a path and she followed it. In a clearing she saw a little house.

Snow White walked to the house. She called out, but no one answered. She found the door open. So she went inside.

There she found a table with seven little chairs. On the table were seven little plates and seven little spoons. Upstairs were seven little beds.

"Seven children must live here!" Snow White thought. "They must be out playing. I'm sure they'd like some nice, hot soup when they come back."

Snow White looked in the pantry. There were carrots, celery, mushrooms, onions, and barley.

Soon, she had cooked a pot full of delicious-smelling soup. She left it on the hearth to simmer.

She was so tired that she went upstairs to take a nap. She lay down on the last little bed and fell sound asleep.

That night, seven little men came down the path to the little house. They stopped short when they saw the open door.

"Someone must be inside!" one of them whispered.

Carefully, they tiptoed into the house. And there, on the hearth, they saw the pot of delicious soup.

"Someone has surely been inside!" another said quietly.

They tiptoed up the stairs. And there, on the last little bed, they saw the sleeping Snow White!

That's when Snow White woke up.

> *What would you do if you were Snow White?*

When Snow White saw the little men, she smiled.

"Why, you're not children at all!" she said.

"Who are you?" asked the leader of the little men.

Snow White told them her sad story. The little men felt very sorry for her.

"I have nowhere to go," Snow White said finally.

The little men excused themselves and went outside to talk things over.

"She must stay with us!" said one.

"But our house is small," said another. "There is no room!"

"We will make room for Snow White," said a third.

And so the little men agreed to ask Snow White to stay. And she said yes.

In return, she promised to cook their meals and keep
their home clean.

"Just beware," they told her. "Never open the door to
strangers!"

And Snow White agreed.

Meanwhile, the woodsman had returned to the castle. He carried the heart of a deer in place of Snow White's heart, to prove to the queen that Snow White was indeed no more.

The wicked queen was very pleased.

But the next morning, when she asked her magic mirror who was the most beautiful in the land, the mirror said, "The loveliest is still Snow White, who lives in a house with seven little men."

The queen fell into a rage. She was determined to do away with Snow White.

So she disguised herself as an old woman. Then she made a poisoned apple. She put the apple in a basket and went to the woods to find Snow White.

The wicked queen is jealous of Snow White. Is that a reason to be mean to her?

Soon, the wicked queen found the little house of the seven little men. She knocked on the door.

Snow White remembered what the little men had said about not opening the door to strangers. So she peeked out the window to see who it was.

"I'm just an old lady selling apples," the wicked queen said.

"I was told never to open the door to strangers," Snow White replied.

The queen was wicked, but she was also smart. She knew how to make Snow White open the door.

"You are a good girl indeed," she told the girl, "and very wise. Of course you should not open the door to me or anyone else. Because you are so clever, I will give you a gift of one of my apples. Here!" And the queen held the bright red poisoned apple out so Snow White could see it.

Snow White could not resist. She opened the door a tiny crack to take the apple. It looked so delicious that she immediately took a bite.

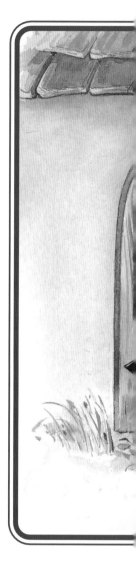

Instantly, the poison did its work. Snow White fell to the ground, lifeless.

The wicked queen laughed. Then she disappeared without a trace.

Meanwhile, the little men were working away at their diamond mine when the sky grew dark and the wind picked up. There was going to be a big storm.

Worried about Snow White being alone in the little house, the men picked up their tools and headed for home.

The clouds kept gathering.

Lightning flashed up ahead.

"There is something wrong," said one little man. "I can feel it in my bones."

"So can I," said another.

They all walked more quickly. They wanted to get home as soon as they could.

Of course, the little men were right. Something was very wrong.

When they got home, they found poor Snow White lying lifeless on the ground.

The little men were grief-stricken. They could not be comforted. They had loved Snow White very much.

They did not want to part with her, so they laid her head on a silk pillow and put her in a glass coffin. That way, they could come and visit her each and every day.

One evening, they saw a young man standing at the coffin, staring down at Snow White.

He was the prince of a nearby kingdom. As soon as he saw her, he instantly fell in love with the silent Snow White.

"May I kiss her?" the prince asked the little men.

Of course, they said yes. So he did.

And as if by magic, Snow White opened her eyes. She had come back to life!

The prince asked Snow White to marry him and come live at his castle. The seven little men were sorry to see her go. But she promised to always come and visit them in their little house.

And that's exactly what she did.

THE FOX AND THE STORK

Once upon a time, a fox invited his friend, a stork, to lunch.

But the sly fox decided to play a trick on her. So, he served up a tasty soup in a flat plate.

No matter how hard she tried, the stork couldn't drink from the flat plate. Her beak was too long and thin.

"I'm afraid I'm not hungry," she said. "I have a terrible headache."

"What a shame!" said the fox, laughing to himself. "The soup is so good!"

"Well, you must let me have you to lunch tomorrow, to return the favor," the stork said.

And the fox agreed to come.

The next day, the fox went to the stork's house.

"I've cooked a special meal for you," she said. "Freshwater shrimp with juniper berries!"

"Mmmm," the fox said, his tummy rumbling. "That sounds good!"

The stork gave the fox a tall jar. "Eat up!" she said.

The fox tried and tried. But his nose could not reach down into the jar.

He had been outsmarted. And the stork had taught him a lesson.

As he tossed and turned hungrily in his bed that night, he sighed. "I'll never try to trick my friends again," he thought.

And he never did.

THE ROOSTER, THE CAT,
AND THE MOUSE

Once upon a time, a little mouse decided to go out and see the world.

After traveling for a long, long way, he came to a farmyard. There, he saw two large animals he had never seen before.

One was quite large and handsome, with four legs. He was covered all over with fur and had long whiskers that gave him a respectable air. This animal was dozing against a wall.

The other animal was terrible to see! It had two legs, red, yellow, and green feathers, and a bad-tempered look. A pair of angry red eyes glared at the little mouse.

"How do you do..." the mouse began. But the creature simply puffed up his chest and screeched a loud, "Cock-a-doodle-doo!"

This scared the little mouse so much that he raced over to a small hole in the wall and dived in.

Inside were three other mice.

"Where did you come from?" they said in amazement.

The little mouse told them his story.

"And I only just escaped from that terrible monster!" he finished. "Where am I now?"

"We are field mice, and this is our home," the other

mice explained. "And you are a very lucky mouse.

"The creature that frightened you is just a rooster. He will not hurt you! But the handsome animal with fur? He is a cat—our deadliest enemy. If he had seen you, he would have gobbled you up!"

And so the little mouse learned a very important rule. You can't always judge someone by the way he or she looks!

THE VAIN CROW

Once there was a crow who met two peacocks in a barnyard.

The peacocks were very beautiful. The crow had never seen such beautiful birds.

"What kind of birds are you?" he asked them.

"We're peacocks," they replied, and one of them spread his tail. Then he screamed, as peacocks do.

The crow flew home, full of admiration. "What fine feathers," he thought. "They must be very happy."

Soon, admiration turned to jealousy. He gazed down at his ugly plumes. "I wish my feathers were as beautiful as the peacocks' feathers," he thought.

Every time he saw his reflection, he became more and more jealous and upset.

One day, when he was visiting the peacocks, he noticed that one of them had dropped a feather. A few weeks later, he found another feather… and then a third, and then a fourth.

When he had the four peacock feathers, he had an idea.

He stuck the peacock feathers on his own tail, using sticky pine resin. Then he paraded around in front of his friends.

"Look at my gorgeous tail," he said. "I'm not ugly like you!"

The crows just laughed. "You're nothing but a crow yourself," they jeered, "even with those flashy feathers."

"You are silly as well as ugly," said the crow. And he decided to leave and go live with the peacocks.

At first, the peacocks thought the crow was another peacock who had just lost most of his feathers, so they were very kind to him.

But soon, the silly crow decided that he wanted to sound like a peacock, too. So he tried to scream the way they did.

Of course, he couldn't. He could only say, "Caw! Caw!"

The peacocks realized that he was just a crow. Furious, they chased him away, pecking the stolen feathers from his tail.

But when the crow tried to return to his friends, he was given the same rough treatment. No one would speak to him.

Which all goes to show: Jealousy can often make a fool of you!

THE GREEDY DOG

Once upon a time, a greedy dog stole a large steak from a butcher's shop. He ran into the woods to eat it.

When he reached the banks of a stream, he happened to see his face reflected in the water. Not realizing that he was looking at himself, he thought he was seeing another dog with a big, juicy steak in his mouth!

"Mmmm," he thought. "If I could get that steak, then I would have two!"

He was a very greedy dog indeed. So he decided that he would bark, to scare the other dog. Then he would jump into the water to get the other dog's steak!

But of course, as soon as he opened his mouth and barked, he dropped his own steak, which disappeared into the water!

And so the greedy dog was left with nothing!

THE HOLE THAT WAS TOO NARROW

Once upon a time, there was a greedy stoat. He would steal food from anyone and eat anything and everything he could.

But he was punished for his greed. One day, he ate some bad eggs that had been lying around in a barn for too long.

He became very ill indeed.

For weeks, he lay between life and death, eating nothing, growing thinner and thinner.

Finally, he began to recover. But had he learned his lesson? No, indeed. He still tried to steal food from everyone. But now he was too weak to do so.

One day, though, his luck changed. He usually didn't go near the town where people lived—it was too dangerous. But this time, he was so hungry that he sneaked close to a tavern that was serving dinner.

Oh, it smelled so good! If only there was something to steal...

Then the stoat saw an incredible thing. There was a crack in the wall. The stoat put his nose to the crack and smelled some delicious smells.

He started to dig. He dug and dug until he made a hole in the wall. Then he looked inside… and oh! What a sight he saw!

He was in the pantry of the tavern. There were hams, salamis, cheeses, honey, jam, and nuts. And it all looked delicious!

The stoat ate and ate. He grew fatter and fatter.

"I will stay here until all the food is gone!" he decided, never thinking of the people who owned the food.

Within a few days, the stoat became so fat that he could not button his trousers.

One afternoon, while he was eating some strawberry jam, the stoat heard a noise. It was the sound of heavy footsteps, climbing down the stairs.

The stoat froze. He needed to escape—right away!

He raced back to the hole he had made. But by now, the stoat was so fat that he couldn't get back out the little hole. In fact, he got stuck!

And that's where the tavern owner found him.

"You robber!" the man said. "I'll deal with you!"

And that was the end of the greedy stoat.

THE MONKEY KING

Once upon a time, there was a jungle where many animals lived together in harmony. Their ruler was a wise old lion.

But one sad day, the lion died, and the animals had to figure out who would be their new king.

They decided that the animal who could fit into the crown would be king.

Each animal tried the crown on. But it fit no one.

Then the silly monkey snatched the crown. He put it around his waist and whirled it round and round.

He threw it high in the air and caught it again and again.

He stood on his head and twirled the crown on the tip of his toes.

The animals laughed and laughed. And finally, they decided to proclaim him king.

Only one animal in the jungle disagreed with their choice. That was the fox.

"That silly monkey can't be our king," he thought. "And I'm going to do something about it!"

One day, the fox just managed to avoid a trap that men had set in the jungle. That gave him an idea.

Do you think the monkey will make a good king? Would you make a good king?

He took the trap to the tree where the monkey lived. He covered the trap with leaves. Then he called up to the monkey.

"Sire!" he cried. "I have a bunch of bananas. I cannot climb up to give them to you. If you come down, you can have them all to yourself—without sharing with anyone!"

The silly monkey scurried down… and was caught in the trap!

Then the fox called to all the other animals.

"Look at our king!" he said. "He was so selfish and in such a hurry, he got caught in a trap. How can we expect him to watch out for us?"

The other animals were persuaded by the fox's clever words. The monkey king lost his crown that very day.

And from then on, the animals in this jungle did without a king. And they did pretty well, too!

THE ANT AND THE CICADA

Once upon a time, during a hot, hot summer, there was a cicada who sang all day long. She sang in the morning and she sang at night.

Nearby, a group of ants were working hard, carrying a load of grain back to their home.

"Why are you working so hard?" the cicada asked.

"We are gathering food for the winter," the ants replied. "When the snow falls, we will have plenty to eat. Why don't you help us?"

"Help you?" the cicada laughed. "I don't think so! Anyway, there's plenty of warm weather left. There's no hurry!"

And so the cicada sang all summer long.

But when winter came and the snow fell, the cicada found herself hungry and alone.

She wandered all over, nibbling on dry stalks of grass.

Finally, she came to the home of the ants.

"Please open the door!" the cicada cried. "I'm very hungry!"

An ant leaned out the window. "Who's there?" she asked.

"It's me!" the cicada replied.

"Ah, I remember you," the ant said. "And what were you doing all summer, when we were working hard to fill our cupboards?"

"I was singing," the cicada replied.

"Singing, eh?" the ant said. "Well, try dancing now!"

> *Do you think the ant will share any of her food with the cicada? Why? What would you do if you were the ant?*

THE FOX AND THE GRAPES

Once upon a time, there was a fox who loved to steal chickens from a local farmer.

All the animals for miles around were afraid of him. He was always hungry, and he was very selfish and proud.

One day, he jumped the high fence around the henhouse. He was just about to pick out a fat hen when the farmer heard the hens cackling. The farmer raced to the henhouse with a broom and hit the fox over the head.

At the same time, the farmer's dogs raced up.

The fox dashed out of the henhouse. He scrambled over the fence with the dogs nipping at his heels. And he didn't stop running until he had reached the woods.

"Whew!" he thought. "That was close."

He was still very hungry. And there was no chance of a chicken supper. And then he saw a bunch of grapes hanging just above his head.

"Well, if there's nothing else," muttered the fox, "I guess I'll eat those grapes."

He started to jump up toward the grapes. But they were just out of his reach.

He jumped and jumped, but he couldn't get them.

"Caw! Caw!" mocked a crow overhead.

The fox did not want to look like a fool. So he looked up and said, "Sour grapes! I'll come back when they're ripe."

> *Do you think the grapes were sour? Why did the fox say they were sour?*

THE HORSE AND THE DONKEY

Once upon a time, there were a horse and a donkey. They lived together in a stable owned by a farmer.

The farmer used the horse to pull his carriage. And although he liked both animals, he treated the horse much better. The horse had better food and carried a lighter load than the hard-working donkey.

But the donkey never complained. He just worked harder.

One day, the farmer was going to market. As usual, he gave the horse two light sacks to carry. The donkey was laden with many heavy bags of grain.

The donkey had grown thin and frail from working so hard. And as he walked along with the horse, he said, "I'm feeling very weak today. Could you please help me, Horse, by carrying some of this grain?"

But the horse looked at the donkey and shook his head. "Why should I help you?" he asked. "Donkeys are beasts of burden. Horses are noble animals! Of course your load should be heavier than mine."

The donkey labored on. But soon, he could not go any further. He fell down in the road.

When the farmer saw this, he felt pity for the poor donkey.

He took all the bags of grain off the donkey's back and gave them to the horse.

The horse shook his head. "I'd have done better to help the donkey when he could walk," he thought. "Then, we would have shared the load. Now I have to carry the whole thing!"

THE HORSE AND THE WOLF

Once upon a time, a horse was grazing in a meadow when a hungry wolf came by.

"That's a nice-looking horse!" the wolf thought. "He'd make a juicy meal! It's a shame he's so big. I don't think I could bring him down. On the other hand… maybe I can trick him!"

So he went as close as he could to the horse. "Good day!" he said pleasantly. "I must say, you're looking rather pale, Mr. Horse."

The horse shook his head. "Pale? Oh, no," he replied. "This is my natural color. I was born white and gray."

The wolf pretended not to understand. "Yes, you're not looking well at all," he went on. "You know, I'm a doctor. If you tell me where the pain is, I can help."

All the while, the wolf was getting closer and closer, looking for a way to attack the horse.

The horse, however, was no fool. "Yes!" he suddenly cried. "Now that you mention it, I have a sore hind foot. It's been swollen for ages. Take a look."

Without thinking, the wolf trotted up to the hoof, which the horse had raised in the air.

As soon as the wolf was in range, the horse gave him a mighty kick, sending him flying.

"Would you like to examine me again?" the horse called to the wolf.

But the wolf, whose head was spinning, had no desire for horse steaks anymore.

And that was the last time he tried to get the better of a horse!

RUMPELSTILTSKIN

Once upon a time, there was a miller who loved to boast and brag. His flour was the finest. His house was the biggest. And his daughter was the most beautiful girl in all the land.

One day, the miller and his daughter were traveling on the road when they came upon the king.

True to his nature, the miller boasted about his flour and house and beautiful daughter. But the king was not impressed.

So the miller said to the king, "Ah, your Majesty! Did you know that my daughter can spin straw into gold?"

The king had had enough of the miller's boasts.

"You must come to the palace tomorrow," he told the miller's daughter. "And we will see…"

Now, the miller's daughter was as bright as she was beautiful.

But she could not spin straw into gold. No one could!

So when she went to the palace the next morning, she was very worried.

She had every reason to be.

The king took her into a room that was full of straw. In the center of the room was a spinning wheel.

"You must spin this straw into gold by tomorrow morning," he told her. "If you do, I will make you my queen. But if you fail... I will imprison you in my dungeons for the rest of your life."

Then he left, locking the door behind him.

Oh, no! How did the miller's daughter get into this mess?

The miller's daughter trembled. "What has my father done?" she thought. "I knew his boasting would do us no good!"

But that night, a strange little man appeared in the room. He was dressed all in red and had a long, white beard.

"What will you give me if I spin all this straw into gold for you?" the little man asked.

"I have very little," said the miller's daughter.

"I'll take that necklace you're wearing," the little man told her.

Now, the necklace had been a gift from the girl's mother. She hated to part with it. But she gave it to the little man. After all, what good would it do her in a dungeon?

"Now, go to sleep," the little man said. "And when you wake, all the straw will have turned to gold."

The girl had nothing to lose. And she was very tired.

So she went into the corner and fell asleep.

When she awoke the next morning and looked around, she could hardly believe her eyes.

All the straw was gone. In its place was gleaming gold!

When the king came to check on her, he was amazed.

"Very good, very good," he said. "But I'm not quite ready to make you my queen."

He had more straw brought to the room.

"If you can spin this straw into gold by tomorrow morning, I will certainly make you my queen then," he promised. "But if not—"

The girl knew what would happen.

The king had promised to marry the girl the day before. Why did he test her again?

That night, the strange little man visited the miller's daughter once again.

"What will you give me this time if I spin all this straw into gold?" he asked her.

"I have this ring," the girl said, taking it off and showing it to him.

"All right," said the little man.

Once again, the miller's daughter went into the corner of the room and fell asleep.

And once again, when she awoke, the straw had been turned to the purest gold.

When the king came to visit her, he was even more amazed.

"Very good, very good," he said.

"It seems the miller was actually telling the truth!"

Then he had the room filled with straw one more time.

"If you spin this straw into gold," he told the girl, "tomorrow I will surely make you my queen."

That night, the miller's daughter was again visited by the strange little man.

"What will you give me this time if I spin all this straw into gold?" he asked her.

The girl sat down in despair on the stone floor. "I have nothing else to give," she said.

"Then," said the little man, "when you and the king are married, you must give me your first-born child."

The miller's daughter had no reason to believe she would ever marry the king. After all, he had broken his promise twice already. So she gave the little man her word.

But the miller's daughter was wrong.

When the king came back the next morning and saw the room filled with gold, he held out his hands to her.

"Now I will make you my queen," he said.

The king married the miller's daughter the very next day. And despite everything, they were quite happy together.

One year later, the queen had a son.

She had completely forgotten her promise to the strange little man.

So she was shocked and saddened when one night, soon after the baby was born, he appeared.

"I have come to collect what was promised to me," he said.

"Oh, please!" cried the horrified queen. "Do not take my baby!"

But the little man was firm. "You promised me your first born, and your first born I will have," he said.

"I will give you gold and jewels!" the queen said, crying bitterly.

"I have no use for gold and jewels," the little man said. But he was moved by her tears.

"All right," he told her. "I will give you three days. If you can guess my name, you can keep your baby. If not... he is mine."

The queen was desperate. She called for the king.

He ordered everyone in the court to look up every name that ever was. And he sent men to all four corners of the kingdom to try to find the little man.

But on the third day, the royal chamberlain came to the queen.

"One of the royal messengers was out in the forest," he told her, "and he saw something strange."

"Bring him to me," the queen commanded.

The man soon appeared. He bowed low.

"What did you see?" the queen asked.

"I was deep in the forest," he told her, "when I heard a noise. So I crept closer to look. There, dancing around in a clearing, was a strange little man with a long white beard."

"Yes?" said the queen eagerly. "What happened then?"

"He started to sing," the man told her. "And this is what he sang:

"The babe is mine, tomorrow morn,
Though I may leave the queen forlorn.
She'll never win my guessing game—
For Rumpelstiltskin is my name!"

"Rumpelstiltskin!" the queen gasped. "That is his name... Rumpelstiltskin!"

The next morning, the little man appeared before the queen.

"So, your Majesty," he said. "Can you guess my name?"

The queen frowned. "Is it... Ruddigore?" she asked.

"No!" the little man said gleefully.

"Is it… Robespierre?"
the queen asked next.

"No!" the little man said again.

"Is it… Rumpelstiltskin?"
the queen said, smiling.

The little man's face grew as red as his hat.
He stamped on the ground in a fury.

"How did you guess?
How did you guess?"
he cried.

Then he disappeared…
and was never seen again.

The queen, the king,
and the little prince
lived happily ever after!

THE OX
AND THE
FROG

Once upon a time, there was a conceited frog.
He never missed an opportunity to show the other
frogs how much better he was than everybody else.

When someone was diving, he had to dive deeper.
When someone hopped, he had to hop higher.

One day, an ox came to drink at the pond.

"He's very large," said one frog. "It would take
hundreds of us frogs to make one of him!"

Now, the conceited frog had been afraid of the
ox, and he had jumped into the water as soon as he
saw him. But after listening to the other frogs, he
had to disagree.

"He's big," said the frog. "But he's not as big
as that."

But nobody was paying attention. So the frog puffed up his chest and announced, "I could easily become as big as that ox. Look!"

The frogs began to laugh. "You're much too little!" they said.

So the frog blew himself up more… and more… and more … until he popped!

There was nothing left of the conceited frog at all!

"It all goes to show you," one frog remarked. "It's better not to have a swelled head!"

What does it mean when we say someone has a "swelled head"? Why do people sometimes act like the conceited frog?

THE STUBBORN GOATS

Once upon a time, there were two mountain goats who wanted to cross a stream. So they each climbed up to a large tree trunk that had fallen across the valley.

The goats met in the middle of the tree trunk. Both of them wanted to get across. But the trunk wasn't wide enough for them to pass one another. And neither of them wanted to give way to the other.

They were very, very stubborn goats.

They began to argue. Then the argument turned to fighting. They banged each other with their horns until they both fell into the river.

Wouldn't it have been much simpler if one of them had been polite enough to let the other one pass?

THE FOX AND THE CROW

Once upon a time, there was a crow who found a large piece of cheese. He flew to a nearby branch to eat it in peace.

Just then, a hungry fox passed beneath the tree. "Mmm," she thought. "I'd love to have that cheese. If only I could figure out a way…"

After a moment or two, she spoke to the crow.

"I must say, you are a handsome bird," she said. "I've never seen a bird so big and strong. And such shiny feathers… and such a regal beak. You certainly must be the king of all the birds!"

Now, when the crow heard this, he flapped his wings with pride.

"And what strong legs you have," the fox went on. "And beautiful eyes. Though I haven't heard your voice, I'm sure you can sing more sweetly than any other bird in the forest.

"O King of the Birds!" the fox then said. "Let me hear your sweet song!"

And the crow, who loved all this flattery, couldn't resist. He opened his mouth wide and cawed!

Of course, when he did so, he dropped the piece of cheese. And the fox gobbled it up!

"Silly crow!" she laughed. "You're the silliest bird I ever met! Thanks for the cheese."

Why did the fox compliment the crow? What lesson did the crow learn (hopefully)?

THE LION AND THE MOUSE

Once upon a time, there was a little mouse. One day, he was scampering through the forest when he came upon a hungry lion.

The lion grabbed the mouse. But the mouse quickly said, "Please don't eat me, your Majesty! If you don't, I will do you a good turn one day."

The lion stared at the tiny mouse. Then he began to laugh. "A tiny mouse thinking he could help a big lion like me?" he said. "What a silly idea! But you have made me laugh… and I'm grateful. So I'm going to let you go."

"Oh, thank you, your Majesty!" said the mouse gratefully. And he disappeared into the forest.

A few days later, the lion fell into a trap. He tried and tried but he couldn't get out. He thought all was lost when he heard a small voice.

"Can I help you, your Majesty?" the voice said.

And looking down, the lion saw the little mouse.

The lion sighed. "I'm afraid there's nothing you can do."

But the lion was wrong.

The little mouse had strong white teeth. He chewed on the net that imprisoned the lion. He chewed, and chewed, and chewed—until the lion was free!

"Never has a lion been so grateful to a little mouse!" the lion declared.

"Well, one good turn deserves another!" the mouse replied.

THE CONFERENCE OF THE MICE

Once upon a time, there was a large cat who lived on farm. She was a good hunter, and all the mice around were afraid of her.

So the mice decided to hold a meeting to try to figure out how to defend themselves. Each mouse had a suggestion as to how to deal with the cat.

"Let's build a large trap!" said one.

"How about poisoning her?" said another.

"We can cut off her claws and teeth!" a third declared.

But none of the mice knew how to do any of these things. Finally, one mouse had a good idea.

"We can tie a bell to her tail!" she said. "That way, we'll always know when she's coming, and we can hide!"

All the mice thought this was a wonderful idea... until an old, wise mouse spoke up.

"And who will tie the bell to the cat's tail?" he wanted to know.

Of course, none of the mice volunteered.

It's not enough just to have a "good" idea, is it? What else do you need?

THE LITTLE GOLD FISH

Once upon a time, a poor fisherman and his wife lived in a small cottage by the sea. Every day, he would take his nets and go fishing for their supper.

"And don't come home empty-handed!" his wife would nag.

One morning, the fisherman caught a little gold fish in his nets. Imagine his surprise when the fish spoke to him!

"Kind fisherman," the fish said, "let me go free. If you do, I'll grant you a wish!"

The fisherman was kind, and so he let the fish go.

Then he went home and told his wife what had happened.

"You fool!" his wife said. "Why didn't you ask for something? Go back to the beach this instant and ask for a new washtub!"

The fisherman went back to the shore and called the fish. The fish appeared immediately, and the fisherman told him what his wife wanted.

"Your wish is granted," said the fish.

And sure enough, when the fisherman went home, there was a new washtub in the cottage. But his wife wasn't satisfied.

"If that little fish has such power, it should be able to give you something much better than a new washtub," she grumbled. "Go back and ask it to give you a new house!"

The fisherman hurried back to the sea once again.

"So, what does your wife want now?" the little fish asked.

"I don't like to ask…" the fisherman said. "But she'd like a big house."

"Your wish is granted," said the fish.

But the house did not
satisfy his wife, either.

"We must ask for more!"
she shouted.
"Tell the fish I want a palace
and jewels and fine clothes!"

So the fisherman hurried
back to the sea once more.
The water of the sea was
looking green and the waves
were rough.

"What does your wife
want *now*?" asked the fish.

"She would like a castle
and jewels and nice clothes,"
said the fisherman. He was
very embarrassed.

"Your wish is granted,"
the fish sighed.

When the fisherman went home, his wife's wish had been granted. There she was in front of a beautiful palace, wearing fine clothes and jewels. But she still wasn't satisfied.

"Go back and ask the fish to make me a queen!" she shouted.

The fisherman didn't want to go... but he loved his wife. So he did.

This time, the sea was dark and stormy.

"What does your wife want *now*?" the fish asked.

"She'd like to be a queen," the fisherman said miserably.

"Go home," said the fish.

And when the fisherman did, the palace had vanished, and his little cottage stood where it always had.

"I should have been pleased with what I had, instead of always wanting more," said his sorry wife.

THE PRINCESS AND THE PEA

Once upon a time, there was a prince who wanted to marry a princess. But his mother, the queen, was very particular.

No matter how many princesses came to the castle, not one of them was good enough for her son.

One night, there was a terrible storm. In the middle of it, someone knocked on the castle gates.

When the queen went to see who it was, she found a young lady standing there.

"I am a princess," the girl said. "My carriage has broken down, and my page and I need shelter. May we please come inside?"

The prince saw the princess and immediately fell in love with her. But the queen was not so sure.

"We must make sure that she is a princess," she decided. And she determined to give the young lady her most difficult test.

She prepared a soft bed for the young lady. It had many, many mattresses. But under the bottom mattress, the queen placed a tiny pea.

Then she showed
the girl to her room.

"If she is not delicate
enough to feel the pea,
she is not a true
princess," the queen
told her son.

The next morning,
the queen asked the
young lady how
she had slept.

"I'm sorry to say,"
the young lady said,
"that I didn't sleep a
wink all night. There
was a terrible lump in
my bed."

The queen was
convinced. Only a true princess could have felt the tiny pea under
all those mattresses!

She gave her son permission to marry.

And the prince and princess lived happily ever after.

HANSEL AND GRETEL

Once upon a time, a poor woodcutter lived with his two children, Hansel and Gretel, in a small cottage.

But his second wife was a heartless woman who hated the children and wanted to get rid of them.

"There is not enough food for us all!" she complained to her husband. "You must take the children into the forest and leave them there. Someone will find them and give them a home."

The woodcutter didn't know what to do. But he finally agreed to her cruel demand.

Luckily, Hansel had overheard his wicked stepmother.

The next morning, the woodcutter led Hansel and Gretel into the forest. But Hansel had filled his pockets with little white pebbles that he found outside the door.

The woodcutter told the children to stay in one spot while he went to chop wood... but he never came back.

What do you think Hansel did with the pebbles he gathered?

Gretel began to cry, but Hansel comforted her.

"Don't worry," he said. "I have dropped the pebbles on the path. We'll follow them and get home safely!"

And when the moon rose, the two children followed the pebbles to their home.

When their stepmother saw that they had returned, she was furious. She locked them in their rooms and gave them nothing but bread and water.

The next day, the woodcutter led Hansel and Gretel further into the forest. This time, Hansel dropped bits of bread behind him.

Once more, the children's father deserted them. But this time, when the moon rose, the children saw that the breadcrumbs were gone. They had been eaten by the birds.

"Oh, no!" Gretel cried. "Now we'll never find our way home!"

"Don't be afraid!" said Hansel. "I'll look after you!"
The next morning, the children started to wander through the forest.
Before long, they came upon a very sweet cottage made of chocolate
and icing, gumdrops and candy.

The starving children immediately began eating pieces of the house. Suddenly, the door opened, and an old woman looked out.

"Who's eating my house?" she cried.

"We're sorry," said Gretel. "But we were so very hungry…"

"Well, then, come in! I will take care of you!" the old lady said. "You've nothing to fear."

But the children had a great deal to fear. The old lady was really a wicked witch with evil plans for the children!

Should Hansel and Gretel trust the strange old woman? Why or why not?

The witch locked Hansel up in a cage. "I will fatten you and cook you for my supper!" she told him. She put Gretel to work cleaning the cottage.

Every day, the witch fed Hansel. And every day, she would feel Hansel's finger to see if he was getting fatter.

But Gretel noticed that the witch was nearly blind. So she gave Hansel a chicken bone. Whenever the witch went to feel his finger, he would hold out the bone instead.

"You're still much too thin!" the witch would say.

Finally, the witch grew tired of waiting for Hansel to get plump.

"See if the oven is hot!" she told Gretel. "It is time to roast your brother!"

But clever Gretel said, "I can't tell if the oven is hot enough."

"Move over!" the witch cried. "I'll check it myself!"

And when the witch bent down to check the oven, Gretel gave her a big push and slammed the oven door shut!

Gretel then freed her brother. The children stayed in the house for many days, eating their fill. Then, one day, they found the witch's golden treasure.

"Let's go home!" Gretel cried.

When they arrived, their father was very happy to see them.

"My mean wife has gone away," he said. "I am sorry that I ever listened to her. Please stay with me. I will never leave you again!"

Hansel showed his father the gold. Now they would always have enough to eat.

THE WISE LITTLE GIRL

Once upon a time, there were two brothers. One was rich and one was poor.

One day, they both set off for the market. The rich brother rode a handsome stallion. The poor brother rode a young mare.

At dusk, they stopped at a small hut. They tied their horses outside and went in to sleep.

Imagine their surprise when, the next morning, there were three horses where there had been two before! The mare had given birth to a foal overnight.

But when the brothers came outside, the foal was standing by the stallion. And the rich brother claimed it for his own.

"Whoever heard of a stallion having a foal!" the poor brother cried. "It was born to my mare!"

But the rich brother disagreed. So the brothers decided to go to town and bring the matter before the judge.

But what they didn't know was that it was a special day. On this day, the emperor himself was judging all the cases!

Each brother presented his case before the emperor. The emperor knew well that the poor brother was right. But he decided to have some fun.

"I can't judge which of you should have the foal," he told them. "So I will give it to whoever can answer the following riddles: What is the fastest thing in the world? What is the fattest? What is the softest? And what is the most precious? You must come to the castle in a week and have the answers ready!"

Neither of the brothers could figure out the riddle. So the rich brother went to his neighbor for help. She was very wise, and she owed him money.

"If you can help me," he told her, "you do not have to pay me back what you owe."

"All right," she said. "Now listen well. The fastest thing in the world is my husband's horse. Nothing can beat it! The fattest is my pig. Such a huge beast has never been seen! The softest is the quilt I made for my bed using my own goose's feathers. And the most precious thing is my three-month-old nephew. I wouldn't trade him for all the gold in the world!"

The rich brother wasn't sure about the woman's answers. But he had to say something to the emperor.

In the meantime, the poor brother was worrying about what he would say to the emperor, too. He worried day and night.

Finally, his little daughter came to him and asked, "Father, what is wrong?"

And he told her of the riddles.

Now, his daughter was only seven, but she was very wise.

"Tell the emperor that the fastest thing in the world is the cold north wind," she told him. "The fattest is the soil in our fields, because it grows food for both people and animals. The softest is a child's touch. The most precious is honesty."

When the two brothers returned to the emperor, he asked them the answers to his riddles. The rich brother's answer made him laugh out loud.

But when the poor brother answered, the emperor was amazed.

"Who gave you these answers?" he asked the poor brother.

"My daughter," the man replied.

"You shall be rewarded for having such a wise daughter," the emperor said. "I will give you the foal and a hundred gold pieces… if… you bring your daughter to me in a week.

"She must appear neither undressed nor dressed, neither on foot nor on horseback, neither bearing gifts nor empty-handed. If she does this, you will have your reward."

The poor brother went home in despair. But his daughter comforted him.

"Bring me a hare and a partridge, alive. And leave everything else to me!" she told him.

So the poor brother did what she asked.

A week later, the man and his daughter appeared before the emperor.

The girl was wearing a fishing net. She rode the hare, and had the partridge in her hand. She was neither undressed nor dressed, neither on foot nor on horseback.

"I said, neither bearing gifts nor empty-handed!" scowled the emperor. At these words, the girl held out the partridge. The emperor reached out to grasp it, but the bird flew away. The third condition had been met.

At this, the emperor was humbled. The wise little girl had done everything he had demanded.

"Is your father very poor?" he asked her.

"Oh, yes," she said. "We live on the hares he catches in the rivers

and the fish

he picks from the trees!"

"Aha!" said the emperor.
"So you are not as wise as you seem! Who ever heard of hares
in rivers and fish on trees?"

"And who ever heard of a stallion having a foal?" the little girl
quickly replied.

At that, the whole court burst out laughing. The poor brother
was immediately given the foal and his hundred gold pieces.

And the emperor proclaimed, "Only in my kingdom could such
a wise little girl be born!"

THE FARMER'S WIFE

Once upon a time, there was a farmer who worked far from home in the field of a rich baron.

One day, he found a bag of gold in the field. But the field belonged to the baron. The farmer knew that if the baron found out about the gold, he would take it for himself.

The farmer also knew something else. If he told his wife about the gold, the whole village would know about it in a day, for she could never keep a secret.

So the farmer came up with a plan.

Before going to work the next day, he bought some donuts, some fish, and a nice rabbit. He put the donuts on a tree, put the fish on the ground, and the rabbit in a fishing net on the bank of the river. He hid the gold under a rock.

Then he went home and said to his wife, "It rained yesterday and the woods are filled with mushrooms. Come with me so we can pick them before anyone else does!"

The man and his wife went to the woods. When they got there, the man ran to his wife, shouting, "Look! A donut tree!" And he pointed to the tree where he had put the donuts.

His wife was astonished.

She was even more astonished when she found fish on the ground instead of mushrooms.

The farmer is doing some very strange things. Can you guess why?

Then her husband found the rabbit in the fishing net.

"Today is our lucky day!" he cried. "We might even find a gold treasure!"

He took his wife to the place he had hidden the gold.

"Here!" he said. "A bag of gold! It *is* our lucky day! Don't tell anyone what has happened here," he warned his wife.

But of course, she could not resist telling. And soon, she had told everyone in the village about the treasure.

When the baron heard the story, he sent for the farmer and his wife.

The farmer stood behind his wife and let her do the talking.

"There was a donut tree!" she told him, waving her arms. "And fish grew out of the ground. A rabbit was swimming in the river!

And then there was gold!"

The baron looked at the farmer. The farmer shrugged.

"Go home, you poor man," the baron said. "I have the same problems with my wife."

What does the baron think about the farmer's wife? Is he right?

THE GOLDEN GOOSE

Once upon a time, there was a woodcutter's son named Tom. He was dreamy and foolish, but he had a very kind heart.

One day, his father sent him out to chop down trees for firewood.

When lunchtime came, Tom sat down to eat. Suddenly, a little old man with a white beard popped out from behind a bush.

"Please, young sir, I am hungry. Won't you give me a bite of food?" he asked.

"Of course!" said Tom. "Here! Here is some bread for you."

The old man ate hungrily. When he was done, he said, "You have been very kind. As a reward, I will tell you a secret. If you look behind that tree, you will find something at its roots that is magical!"

And with that, the old man vanished!

Tom did as he was told. And there, among the roots, sat a Golden Goose.

"My, my!" said Tom. He tucked the Golden Goose under his arm and set off for home.

> *What do you think could be so magical about the Golden Goose?*

It was dark by the time he reached a village. There, he went to a tavern. The innkeeper's daughter brought him a bowl of soup.

Tom shared his soup with the Golden Goose. The girl was amazed and asked why he was so kind to his goose.

"It's a magic goose," said Tom proudly. "Be sure to give me a room with a good lock, for I don't want to be robbed."

The girl told her two sisters about the Golden Goose. They decided to steal it. Later, the three tiptoed to Tom's door and opened it with a master key.

The first sister tried to grab one of the Golden Goose's tail feathers, but her hand stuck to the goose. The others tried to pull her sister free, and they became stuck to each other!

The next morning, Tom awoke to find the three sisters sitting on the floor with one hand on the goose.

"Help us. We're stuck to your goose!" wailed the sisters.

"There's nothing I can do," said Tom. "My goose and I are leaving. You'll just have to come along."

The innkeeper saw Tom going out the door with his three daughters. He grabbed the last one—and became stuck himself! His wife grabbed onto him, only to find herself stuck, too.

Before long the village pastor, the baker, and a passing soldier had joined the parade. Tom walked along, paying no attention to their shouting. Soon, a laughing crowd had gathered.

Near the village stood a king's castle. The king's only daughter was pining away, and no doctor could cure her sadness. The king had sworn that any man who made the princess laugh would have her hand in marriage.

The princess had chosen that very morning to drive through the village square. Hearing the laughter, she looked out the carriage window. There was Tom, solemnly marching along with his goose and his strange parade.

The princess started to giggle. Then she laughed. She laughed and laughed. She laughed all the way back to the castle.

The king was overjoyed. He told Tom of his promise. Tom let go of the Golden Goose and took the princess's hand. The goose disappeared with a squawk, and everyone became unstuck.

Tom and the princess were married that very day. So you see, an act of kindness can bring something wonderful and magical to your life.

CHICO AND THE CRANE

In the city of Florence there once lived a nobleman named Sir
Charles. He was famous for his banquets and his love of hunting.

One day, he caught a fine crane. While Chico, the cook, was roasting the bird for a banquet, a pretty maid passed through the kitchen. The roast smelled so delicious that she begged Chico to give her a leg for her supper.

When the roast crane was served to Sir Charles, he immediately summoned Chico.

"Where is the crane's other leg?" he demanded.

"Sire, cranes have only one leg," said Chico.

"Nonsense!" said the nobleman. "We will soon see."

Sir Charles took Chico and his other attendants to the river. As they rode along, Chico saw a flock of cranes asleep, all standing on one leg.

"There, Sire. I was right!" cried Chico. "Cranes have only one leg!"

"Is that so?" replied Sir Charles. He clapped his hands. The birds rose in the air. Everyone could see that they had two legs.

"But, Sire," said the quick-witted cook, "if you had clapped your hands at the table yesterday, the roast bird would have uncurled its other leg!"

Chico is clever, isn't he? But do you think Sir Charles believes him?

THE MUSICIANS OF BREMEN

Once upon a time, there was an old donkey who was treated badly by his master. He had heard that the town of Bremen was looking for singers for its town band. So he decided to run away to Bremen. Surely the band would want someone like him, with his fine, braying voice!

As he went along the road, the donkey met a skinny dog. "Come with me," the donkey said. "If you have a good bark, I'm sure you can find a job with the band, too!"

A little while later, they were joined by an old cat who could no longer catch mice. Then they passed a farmyard. Standing on a fence was a rooster who was crowing to the skies.

"Woe is me!" he crowed. "My master wants to cook me in his pot!"

"Then run away with us," the donkey said. "With a voice like yours, you'll be famous in Bremen!"

Night fell and the four friends found themselves in the dark. As they neared Bremen, they saw a light. It came from a little cottage.

The four crept up to the window ledge. The dog jumped on the donkey's back, the cat climbed onto the dog, and the rooster flew on top of the cat to see what was going on inside.

There, at a table, was a gang of thieves, eating and drinking and celebrating their latest robbery.

The donkey was so hungry that he leaned forward. The dog, the cat, and the rooster fell in through the window.

The barking dog, snarling cat, screeching rooster, and braying

donkey scared the robbers so much that they quickly ran away.

And the four friends happily gobbled up all the food.

Later, the bandits crept back to the cottage to find out what had happened. One of them quietly opened the door to look around.

The cat heard the door open. Startled, she sank her claws into the bandit's back. The dog bit him. The donkey kicked him out the door. And the rooster crowed and crowed.

"Run for your lives!" the bandit cried. "There is a horrible witch inside! She scratched me and bit me and beat me with her stick!"

The bandits fled into the night, never to return to Bremen.

The four friends took over the cottage, where they lived happily for many a year, and sang every day!

THE THREE WISHES

Once upon a time, a woodcutter was about to cut down a tree in the forest when out popped an elf.

"You can't cut this tree down!" the elf cried. "It's my home!"

"I can cut down any tree I want!" said the woodcutter.

"All right!" the elf said. "If you don't cut down this tree, I'll grant you three wishes. Agreed?"

"Agreed!" the woodcutter exclaimed. And then he rushed home to tell his wife.

"Wife! Wife!" he cried when he arrived home. "You'll never guess! I saw an elf in the forest, and he granted me three wishes!"

"Well, we must think about what to wish for!" the wife declared.

So she poured the woodcutter a mug of cider, and they sat down at the table to decide.

The woodcutter took a sip.

"Mmm, this is good," he told his wife.

"I only wish we had a string of sausages to go with it!" she sighed.

And suddenly... a string of sausages appeared out of thin air!

"What have you done?" the woodcutter cried. "You've used up our first wish! You foolish woman. I wish those sausages would stick to your nose!"

And in a second, the sausages had jumped up and stuck to the end of the woman's nose.

"Oh, no!" she wailed. "Our second wish is all gone!"

The woodcutter looked at his wife, and he couldn't help smiling. "If only you knew how silly you looked!" he said.

His wife frowned. Then she tried to pull the sausages off her nose. But they were stuck fast. "Oh, dear!" she wailed again. "These sausages will be on my nose for the rest of my life! Pull them off, husband! Pull them off!"

But no matter how hard he tried...

...the woodcutter could not pull the sausages off his wife's nose!

"What shall we do?" the woodcutter asked his wife. But they both knew the answer.

"I wish..." he said sadly, thinking of all the riches that they could have wished for. "I wish that these sausages were off my wife's nose."

And just like that, the sausages fell off her nose and onto the table.

The woodcutter hugged his wife. "Perhaps we will be poor," he told her. "But we will be happy again!"

"And," his wife replied, her eyes twinkling, "we can have these nice sausages for supper!"

WHAT OTHER PEOPLE THINK

Once upon a time, a farmer and his son went to market to sell a donkey. The farmer decided to carry the donkey in his wheelbarrow. This way, the donkey would fetch a better price, since it wouldn't look tired and dusty.

But as they walked along, the people they passed laughed and sneered at them.

"Look at that foolish man!" they said. "Wheeling a donkey in a wheelbarrow! How silly can you get?"

Finally, the farmer had heard enough. He took the donkey out of the wheelbarrow, climbed on his back, and went on.

This time, the people they passed pointed and said, "Look at that cruel man! He is riding his donkey while his poor little boy runs behind him, trying to keep up!"

This confused the farmer.

"What am I to do?" he thought. Finally, he got off the donkey and let his son ride.

This time, the people who saw them said, "It's a disgrace. That healthy young man is riding, while his tired old father must go on foot!"

The farmer scratched his head. Then, in the end, he and his son both got onto the donkey.

This time, the people who saw them said, "What heartless people! Two people on one little donkey!"

The farmer threw up his hands in disgust.

"That's it!" he cried. "From now on, I'll do things my way, and pay no attention to what anyone else thinks!"

And that's exactly what he did.

PINOCCHIO

Once upon a time, a carpenter found a strange log of oak while mending a table.

When he began to cut it, he thought he heard the wood crying. So he decided to get rid of it.

He gave it to his friend, the shoemaker Geppetto, who wanted to make a puppet.

Geppetto started to carve the wood into the figure of a boy. "I'll call him Pinocchio," he decided.

Suddenly, he heard a voice. "Ooh! That hurt!"

Geppetto was amazed. He carved the head, then the eyes. They stared back at him!

Then he carved the nose and the mouth. And no sooner was the mouth finished than the puppet began to laugh!

"Be still!" said Geppetto.

He finished the puppet's arms and legs. As soon as the hands were done, Pinocchio grabbed the wig off Geppetto's head and put it on his own.

Then he stuck out his tongue at the astonished man.

"You naughty boy!" said Geppetto. "Making fun of your own father!"

Geppetto was a kind man, and he did not stay angry long. Before long, he had taught Pinocchio to walk.

But as soon as Pinocchio learned how, he ran out the door and into the street.

"Stop him! Stop him!" shouted Geppetto.

Luckily, a policeman heard the shoemaker's shouts. He quickly grabbed Pinocchio.

"I'll box your ears!" gasped Geppetto. But that wasn't possible, for he had forgotten to make ears for the puppet. So he carved Pinocchio a pair of ears.

"I'm sorry, Father," said Pinocchio as soon as he could hear.

Geppetto forgave him. Then he made him a flowered jacket, some trousers, some shoes of bark, and a hat.

"Thank you!" said Pinocchio, hugging his father. "Now, I'd like to go to school so I can help you when you're old."

"That's very nice," said Geppetto. "But we don't have enough money to buy you a school book."

Pinocchio was very sad. So Geppetto got up, put on his old coat, and left the house. When he came back, he was carrying a book, but his coat was gone.

"Where's your coat, Father?" Pinocchio asked.

"I sold it because I was warm," he fibbed.

"You are a very good father," Pinocchio told him.

The next morning, Pinocchio set out for school. He meant to learn a lot so he could go to work and buy Geppetto a new coat.

But on the way, he heard the sound of a brass band. He forgot all about school.

"What's going on?" Pinocchio asked.

"It's a puppet show!" a man told him.

A puppet show? Pinocchio had to see it! But it cost four pennies to get in.

So Pinocchio sold his book for four pennies and hurried in to see the show.

When Pinocchio got inside, all the puppets started to shout.

"Come join us, Pinocchio!" they called. And so he did!

Pinocchio sold his school book to get into the puppet show! How do you think that will make his father feel? Why?

Suddenly, the puppet master opened the curtains. He was very large with a long beard and bushy eyebrows.

"What's going on here!" he roared. "Stop that noise or you'll have to answer to me!"

That night, the puppet master found that the stove needed more wood.

He was about to throw Pinocchio into the oven, but the puppet burst into tears. "I will never see my father again!" he sniffed.

"You have a father?" asked the man, astonished.

"Yes," Pinocchio said. And he told the man his story.

The puppet master looked very mean. But he had a soft place in his heart.

He gave Pinocchio five gold pieces. "Give these to your father," he said. "Tell him to buy a new coat."

Pinocchio thanked him and left for home.

But on the way, he came upon a cat and a fox.

Pinocchio was so happy that he told them of his good fortune.

The two stared greedily at the gold coins.

"If you'd really like your father to be happy," said the fox, "I know a field where you can plant those coins. Tomorrow, there will be ten times as many!"

The wooden boy believed the fox, so he started off for the field so he could bury the coins. While he walked, he put the coins under his tongue to keep them safe.

But on the way, he met two hooded shapes. "Your money or your life!" growled one. It sounded an awful lot like the fox.

Pinocchio couldn't speak, because of the coins in his mouth. And when the two villains couldn't find his gold, they hung him on a tree.

Then they disappeared.

Luckily, as Pinocchio was hanging there, a beautiful fairy with blue hair happened to pass by.

"Whatever happened to you?" she asked.

Of course, Pinocchio still couldn't answer because of the coins.

The fairy clapped her hands for her pet woodpeckers. The birds soon came and pecked the rope to pieces.

Thump! Pinocchio sat down hard. He nearly swallowed the coins. He quickly put them in his pocket.

Then the fairy took him home and put him to bed.

She had the doctor and his assistants in to check on Pinocchio. They had never seen a wooden boy before, and they didn't know what to do to help him.

So the fairy gave him a drink of a special magic potion. It made him feel much better.

"So, tell me," the fairy said. "What happened to you?"

Pinocchio told her his story. But he left out the part about selling the book.

Suddenly, his nose began to get longer and longer.

"What's happening?" he cried, terrified.

The fairy laughed. "You are telling lies," she said. "I can tell because your nose is growing."

She clapped her hands again. This time, the woodpeckers came and pecked Pinocchio's nose down to its normal size.

"Now, always tell the truth," she told him. "And go straight home to your father."

But foolish Pinocchio went back to the field.
He still believed what the fox had told him!
He buried the coins under a tree.
Then he waited by a bush until dawn.
But when he went back to dig up
the coins, he found an empty hole.

What do you think happened to the coins?

Pinocchio sadly went home. But Geppetto was happy to see him, and forgave him completely.

The next day, the wooden boy went off to school.

Unfortunately, he made friends with Wick, the laziest boy in the class.

"I am quitting school and going to Toyland. Why don't you come with me?" said Wick. "Nobody ever studies there, and you can play all day long!"

"Is there really such a place?" asked Pinocchio.

"Of course!" said Wick. "Meet me at midnight. That's when the coach arrives to take us to Toyland!"

Silly Pinocchio met Wick. Sure enough, at midnight, the coach arrived. It was pulled by a row of sad little donkeys wearing boots.

But Pinocchio didn't notice that. He was too excited to be going to Toyland!

Toyland was just like Wick said it would be. Pinocchio loved it!

"I was right, wasn't I?" said Wick.

But one day, when Pinocchio woke up, he got a horrid surprise.

When he looked in the mirror, he found he had sprouted a long pair of hairy donkey's ears!

The next day, they were even longer.

Pinocchio pulled on a cap and went to look for Wick. Wick, too, was wearing a hat that was pulled down to his nose.

The two boys stared at each other. Then they both pulled their hats off.

"You look so funny!" cried Wick. "Ha ha ha ha ha!"

But suddenly, the "ha ha has" turned to "hee-haws"! Then Wick fell to his hands and knees.

"Pinocchio, help!" he cried. But Pinocchio couldn't help. The same thing was happening to him.

Pinocchio and Wick were turning into donkeys!

When the Toyland wagon driver heard the braying of his new donkeys, he rubbed his hands with glee.

"Two fine new donkeys for market," he said. "I'll get at least four gold pieces for them! Maybe the animal trainer at the circus will buy them, and make them jump through hoops!"

This was the terrible fate that awaited all the boys who played hooky and went to Toyland!

It would have been better if Pinocchio stayed at school. Do you think he'll be a donkey for the rest of his life?

But Pinocchio wasn't sold to the circus. He was sold to a tanner—a man who made leather.

When Pinocchio wouldn't pull the tanner's cart, the tanner decided to kill him and turn his donkey skin into leather.

He took Pinocchio to the edge of a cliff.

As Pinocchio looked down at the water, the tanner pushed the poor donkey over the edge.

Pinocchio struggled to swim. As he thought sadly of his father, a school of little fish appeared and began to nibble away at his donkey skin.

Soon, he was a little wooden boy again!

Just as the fish had finished, Pinocchio felt himself being hauled up by the leg.

"Where's my donkey skin?" gasped the farmer.

"That was me!" laughed Pinocchio, slipping his foot out of the rope. "The fish have your donkey skin!"

"I'll sell you for firewood!" cried the man.

"No, you won't!" said Pinocchio. And he jumped back into the water.

> *Pinocchio got away!—but what do you think will happen to him now?*

At that moment, a huge whale glided by. His jaws were open wide, so he could catch any food that happened across his path.

"Help!" cried Pinocchio, swimming as hard as he could. But a wave washed him into the whale's mouth.

Down, down he went through the whale's huge throat.

When Pinocchio came to his senses, everything was dark.

"Help! Won't anybody save me?" he cried.

Suddenly, he saw a flickering candle.

It sat on a table. And there was a chair—could it be?

It was his father, Geppetto!

Sobbing for joy, they hugged each other. Then Geppetto told Pinocchio how he came to be in the whale's stomach.

"I have been searching everywhere for you," Geppetto explained. "Finally, I made a boat so I could search in other lands. But the boat sank in a storm, and here I am!"

"We must escape!" said Pinocchio.

"But how?" Geppetto asked.

Pinocchio and Geppetto climbed out of the whale's stomach and into his throat. Then they carefully walked up to his tongue.

When a drop of hot candle wax dripped onto the whale's tongue, the whale quickly spat out Pinocchio and Geppetto!

Luckily, they were near a beach. They swam to the shore.

There, they found a small hut and they rested. But Geppetto was ill and weak from hunger. So Pinocchio took him home.

The puppet then went to work. He rose early each morning to care for Geppetto. He wove baskets into the night to earn money for Geppetto's food.

Soon, Geppetto was well again.

One night, Pinocchio had a dream. In his dream, the blue fairy came to reward Pinocchio for what he had done for Geppetto.

The next morning, when Pinocchio woke up… he was a real boy!

Geppetto hugged his son happily.

"What happened to my old wooden self?" Pinocchio wondered.

"Look there!" exclaimed Geppetto, pointing to a a chair.

"I couldn't carve a heart for the old Pinocchio," Geppetto said, smiling. "But because of your hard work and kindness, you have made one for yourself!"

And Pinocchio and Geppetto lived happily ever after!

THE PIED PIPER OF HAMELIN

Adapted from the poem by Robert Browning

Once upon a time, there was a town in Germany called Hamelin. The people who lived in Hamelin were honest and kind. But years went by, and the town grew rich and greedy. The people cared for nothing but their gold.

One day, something very strange happened. Rats came to the town of Hamelin. There were rats in the barns and rats in the houses. There were rats everywhere! The town brought in more cats, but the rats chased *them* from town!

The people of Hamelin went to the mayor and demanded that he do something.

The mayor assured them he would get rid of the rats. Just then there was a knock on the door. When the mayor opened it, a man stood there.

He wore bright striped trousers and a blue cape. He had a red hat on his head with a blue feather. He carried a long golden flute.

"I am the Pied Piper," he said. "For a hundred pieces of gold, I'll rid your town of its rats."

"We'll give you five hundred if you can do it!" cried the mayor.

"One hundred will do," said the stranger.

Early the next morning, the sweet sounds of a flute could be heard around Hamelin. The Pied Piper walked along the street. And from every barn and every farm, from every hole and every home, the rats came out. Called by the music, they followed the Pied Piper down the streets of the town. They followed him all the way to the river.

The Pied Piper walked to the middle of the river. And the rats followed him in and drowned.

By that evening, there were no rats left in Hamelin.

But the people of Hamelin, as you'll recall, were very greedy. So when the Pied Piper came to collect his reward, they offered him just ten gold pieces.

"After all," said the mayor, "it clearly wasn't very difficult to get the rats to leave."

"One hundred gold pieces, or you will be sorry," the Pied Piper said quietly.

But the mayor shook his head.

"Then see what happens when you break a promise," said the Pied Piper.

The next morning, once again the sound of the Piper's sweet music could be heard throughout the town.

But this time, all the children heard it.

One by one, they crept out of their houses and followed the Piper.

They followed him out of the town. They followed him up a mountain and into a large cave.

One boy walked very slowly with a crutch. But even he followed after the Pied Piper.

The boy could see that inside the cave was a magical world full of wonders. He wanted to go inside. But he wasn't quick enough. By the time he got there, the cave had vanished... along with the other children.

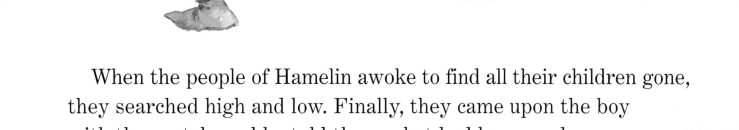

When the people of Hamelin awoke to find all their children gone, they searched high and low. Finally, they came upon the boy with the crutch, and he told them what had happened.

"We were too greedy," the mayor said sadly.

The children were never seen again. But there is a legend that far away, beyond the mountain, is a town of kind, happy people. And these people are the children of the children of Hamelin.

THE SNOW QUEEN

Adapted from the original story by Hans Christian Andersen

Once upon a time, there was a magic mirror. It had been made by an evil magician. In this mirror, love looked like hate.

One day, the mirror broke into a thousand pieces. The pieces flew all over the world. If a sliver of the mirror entered someone's eye or heart, that person became cold and hateful.

Carl and Gerda were two young children who loved each other very much.

Carl had a sweetpea vine that grew on his windowsill. It twined with the rose that grew on Gerda's sill.

That was how much they loved one another.

One day, Carl was looking out the window at the falling snow. And suddenly, one of the snowflakes turned into a beautiful young woman with a crown on her head.

"Come with me, Carl!" she whispered.

Then Carl felt something prick his eye. He didn't know it, but it was a piece of the magic mirror.

But after the sliver of mirror entered his eye, Carl changed. He became rude and hateful. Gerda alone still loved him with all her heart, although he was mean to her.

Often, because none of the other children liked him, Carl would play by himself.

One day, when he was playing alone in the snow, he heard the sound of jingling bells.

He looked up. There was the beautiful woman again. This time, she wore a coat with a big fur collar, and sat in a fur-lined sleigh drawn by a large white horse. Carl didn't know it, but this was the dreaded Snow Queen.

"Tie your sled to my sleigh and come with me!" she called merrily. "We'll have a wonderful ride!"

Carl was enchanted and did what she asked.

But soon the Snow Queen's sleigh rose into the sky. Carl was frightened, but there was nothing he could do.

They landed in a cold white field. "Come here and keep warm!" the Snow Queen told Carl. And then she kissed him on the forehead.

As her icy lips touched his skin, Carl's heart froze. He forgot all about Gerda and his home life.

But Gerda did not forget Carl.

The next spring, Gerda went down to the river. She got into a little boat, hoping the river would take her to her friend.

As the sun set, the boat came to rest on the shore of a forest. Gerda climbed out. A reindeer came through the trees, and a crow flew down and sat on a branch.

"If you're looking for Carl," the crow said, "I saw him fly by on the Snow Queen's sleigh."

"Where is he now?" Gerda cried.

"I will take you to him," the reindeer kindly told her.

Could you still love Carl
as much as Gerda does?

Gerda climbed onto the reindeer's back, and it galloped off.
Soon, they came to a frozen land far, far in the north.

There on a hill was the Snow Queen's castle. In front of the
castle, sitting on a rock, was Carl. He was staring straight ahead.
For, of course, his heart was frozen.

"Carl!" called Gerda. But he did not answer.

Gerda threw her arms around Carl and burst into tears.

Her tears fell onto his eyes and over his chest. They melted his frozen heart, and he, too, began to cry. And when he cried, the horrible sliver of mirror floated out of his eye, and he remembered everything.

Carl especially remembered how he loved his friend, Gerda. The reindeer soon flew them back to their homes.

And Carl was forever grateful to Gerda and her faithful love and kindness.

DOPEY DENNIS

Once upon a time, there was a boy named Dennis. Everybody called him Dopey Dennis... and you will soon see why.

Dennis lived with his mother in a nice house with a vegetable garden and a henhouse. One day, his mother had to go to town. She left Dennis in charge.

"The hen is sitting on her eggs," his mother told him. "Make sure nobody goes near her. And keep the house tidy."

When Dennis's mother had gone, Dennis went to the henhouse to watch over the hen. Soon, the hen got up to stretch her legs.

"Get back on those eggs!" Dennis yelled.

The hen, of course, didn't understand him. She just clucked.

So Dennis picked up a stick and waved it at her.

Unfortunately, he frightened her and the poor hen ran off.

"Oh, dear!" Dennis thought. "Who will sit on the eggs now? I guess I have to!"

So Dennis sat on the eggs. But of course, they broke. When he got up, his trousers were all sticky.

"I'm in trouble now," he thought. "But I know what I can do. I'll make Mother some lunch. Then she won't be angry with me."

Dennis put a duck on a spit to roast. Then he went to the basement to draw some grape cider from a barrel.

At that moment, there was a terrible noise in the kitchen. Dennis rushed upstairs to see what it was… forgetting to turn off the tap on the cider barrel.

When Dennis got to the kitchen, he saw the cat with the roast duck in her mouth. "Stop, thief!" he cried.

He chased the cat around and around the house. He smashed plates, glasses, and vases, overturned chairs, and made a terrible mess. At last, the cat dropped the duck and jumped out the window.

Dennis put the duck on the table and went to get the cider. But when he got downstairs, he saw about six inches of grape cider on the floor.

"Oh, dear!" Dennis thought. "What am I to do now?"

Dennis thought and thought. Suddenly he had an idea. There were bags of flour in the cellar. He opened one, two, three, four, five bags of flour and scattered it over the floor.

"The flour will absorb the cider," he thought.

And so it did... making a sticky paste that stuck to Dennis's shoes. When Dennis got the jug of cider and carried it upstairs, he left grape cider-and-flour footprints everywhere.

The more Dennis thought of the mess he had made, the more he was afraid his mother would scold him. So he decided to hide.

Some time later, his mother returned. When she saw the broken plates, glasses, and vases, the overturned chairs, and the red footprints, she became frightened.

"Dennis, where are you?" she cried.

Then she saw a pair of legs sticking out of the oven.

"I'm not surprised that you're hiding from me," she said to Dennis, shaking her head. "While I'm cleaning up this mess, you can take this bolt of cloth to market. Be sure to get a good price for it."

"I will," said Dennis. And he left for the market.

When Dennis got to the market, he began to shout:

"Who will buy this lovely cloth?"

A number of women went over to ask him about it.

"How much is it?" asked one.

"Is it soft?" asked another.

"Will it last a long time?" asked a third.

"I won't sell my cloth to chatterboxes," Dennis told them, and off he went.

He walked for a while. Then, in the middle of the town square, he saw the statue of a man. Thinking it was a fine gentleman, he said, "Sir, would you like to buy my cloth?"

The statue didn't answer.

"All right," said Dennis. "I'm glad you are not a chatterbox. If you don't answer, that means you want to buy it. Isn't it beautiful? Don't you like it?"

Of course, the statue said nothing.

Dennis thought that meant he wanted the cloth. So he left it beside the statue and went home. When he got there, his mother asked him how much money he had gotten.

"Oh, no!" cried Dennis. "I forgot to ask him for money. I'll go back and get it now."

> *Does Dennis's mother think he messes up on purpose? Do you?*

Dennis went back to the square. But the cloth was gone.

"I see you've taken the cloth home already," he told the statue. "Fine. Now, pay me for it!"

But of course, the statue still said nothing.

"This is very unfair!" Dennis shouted. "You owe me money for the cloth!"

But the statue was silent.

Dennis became so angry that he picked up a stick and hit the statue on the head.

The statue's head fell off. Out of it poured a handful of gold coins that had been hidden there many years before.

Dennis picked up the coins, put the head back on the statue, and went home.

"Look, Mother! Look at how much he paid me!" Dennis cried.

His mother was amazed.

"Who gave you such a good price?" she asked him.

"A man who kept his money in his head," Dennis replied.

"Dennis!" his mother said. "You frightened away the hen, broke the eggs, flooded the cellar with cider, wasted five bags of flour, overturned chairs, and smashed plates, glasses, and vases. If you think you're going to lie to me as well, you're badly mistaken." And she chased him out of the house.

"Now go weed the vegetable garden!" she called. "I don't want to see you until suppertime!"

But Dennis just sat in front of the house.

So his mother grabbed the first thing that was handy— a basket of dried figs and raisins— and threw it at him.

"Mother! Come quick!" Dennis cried. "Bring a basket! It's raining figs and raisins!"

His mother shook her head. "What am I to do with a boy like him?" she sighed.

In the next few days, Dennis boasted about the gold coins all over town. Soon, the town judges heard the tale and sent for him.

"Who gave you these coins?" they asked.

"The gentleman who's always standing in the town square," Dennis told them.

"But that is a statue!" the judges cried.

"He didn't tell me his name," Dennis said. "Maybe it is Mr. Statue. Anyway, he kept his money in his head."

The judges stared at each other in astonishment. Then one of the judges asked, "Dennis. What day did the man pay you the gold?"

"The day it rained figs and raisins!" Dennis answered cheerfully.

The judges shook their heads. Dennis was truly dopey, they decided.

"Go on home," they told him.

So Dennis went home and lived happily with his mother.

Did the judge believe Dennis? What would you think?